EDGE
BOOKS

Top Hybrid Dogs

PUGGLE

Pugs
Meet
Beagles!

by Sue Bradford Edwards

CAPSTONE PRESS
a capstone imprint

Edge Books are published by Capstone Press,
1710 Roe Crest Drive, North Mankato, Minnesota 56003
www.mycapstone.com

Library of Congress Cataloging-in-Publication Data
Names: Edwards, Sue Bradford, author.
Title: Puggle : pugs meet beagles! / by Sue Bradford Edwards.
Description: North Mankato, Minnesota : Edge Books, an imprint of Capstone
    Press, [2019] | Series: Top hybrid dogs | Includes bibliographical
    references and index. | Audience: Age 8-14. | Audience: Grade 7 to 8.
Identifiers: LCCN 2018036900 (print) | LCCN 2018037747 (ebook) | ISBN
    9781543555301 (ebook) | ISBN 9781543555202 (hardcover : alk. paper)
Subjects: LCSH: Puggle--Juvenile literature. | Designer dogs--Juvenile
    literature.
Classification: LCC SF429.P92 (ebook) | LCC SF429.P92 E39 2019 (print) | DDC
    636.76--dc23
LC record available at https://lccn.loc.gov/2018036900

Editorial Credits
Editor: Maddie Spalding
Designer and Production Specialist: Laura Polzin

Photo Credits
Alamy: Purestock, 19; iStockphoto: Debrock44, 10, happyborder, cover, stu99, 29;
Newscom: Picani imageBroker, 15; Shutterstock Images: anetapics, 16–17, 22, Anna
Hoychuk, 12–13, 23, Elizabeth Winterbourne, 20 21, everydoghasastory, 7, 26–27,
Igor Normann, 17, Lipsett Photography Group, 4–5, Mary E. Cioffi, 24–25, Utekhina
Anna, 8–9

Design Elements
bittbox

Printed in the United States of America.
PA48

TABLE OF CONTENTS

CHAPTER ONE

MEET THE PUGGLE

How do you have fun with dogs? Do you like to explore the neighborhood together? Do you enjoy cuddling at the end of the day? If you like these activities, a puggle might be the right fit for your family.

Puggles are adorable dogs that have the floppy ears of a beagle and the wrinkly face of a pug. These little dogs love to run and play. They have a lot of energy, but they also enjoy cuddling up with their owners. These qualities make the puggle the top choice for many families.

Puggles are friendly dogs.

Puggles are a type of hybrid dog. A hybrid dog is a cross between two **breeds**. The breeds are usually chosen for certain traits, or qualities. A puggle is a cross between a pug and a beagle. Pugs and beagles are **purebred** dogs. Puggles get traits from both of these breeds. Puggles might have a pug's light brown fur and curly tail. They might also have a beagle's floppy ears and playful nature. There's a lot to love about these cute little dogs.

Fact Box

Puggles are not the only pug hybrid. A chug is a pug and Chihuahua hybrid. A daug is a pug and dachshund hybrid. A pug-zu is a pug and shih tzu hybrid.

 breed – a type of dog that has specific traits

purebred – a dog that is the same breed as its parents

Hybrid Vigor

A hybrid dog is different from a mutt. A mutt is a mix of many breeds. Often no one knows which ones. A hybrid combines only two breeds that are chosen carefully. The breeds are often chosen to avoid certain health problems. Breeding for improved health is called hybrid vigor. Yet some **breeders** believe hybrid vigor is a myth. They think that purebred dogs are just as healthy as hybrids.

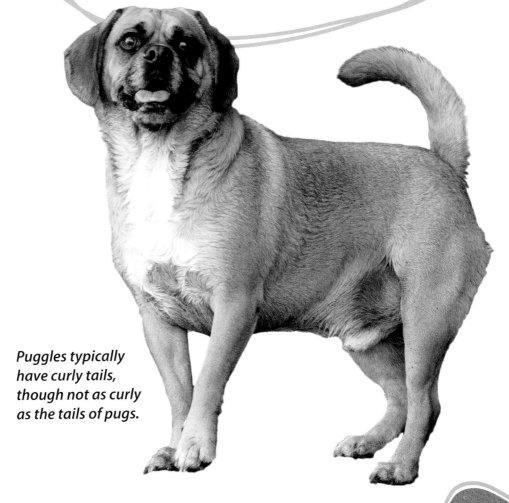

Puggles typically have curly tails, though not as curly as the tails of pugs.

breeder – someone who brings dogs together so they can breed, or reproduce

CHAPTER TWO

PUGGLE HISTORY

The puggle's parents are among the most popular dog breeds. Pugs were first bred in China in about 400 BC. They were companion dogs for wealthy people. Today pugs are still bred as pets.

Beagles are a type of dog called a hound. Hound dogs are bred for hunting. Beagles can track down animals such as rabbits. Beagles were popular hunting dogs in England in the 1500s. Today beagles are also bred as pets.

No one is certain where or when the first **litter** of puggle puppies was born. A breeder named Wallace Havens was the first to call these dogs puggles. He bred puggles at Puppy Haven Kennels in Madison, Wisconsin, in the 1980s.

 litter – a group of puppies born from the same mother

Pugs have been bred as pets for thousands of years.

Havens was the first breeder to register puggles with the American Canine Hybrid Club. If someone wants a hybrid puppy, this group can tell the person which breeders have hybrid puppies.

At first puggles were not very popular. People laughed when Havens mentioned crossing a beagle with a pug. They thought the idea of a pug and a beagle mix seemed odd. But Havens believed this hybrid dog would make a good family pet. So he kept breeding puggles.

The puggle's adorable appearance helped make it a popular pet.

Fact Box

A puggle with a beagle mother and a pug father is called a first-generation puggle. A puggle with puggle parents is called a second-generation puggle.

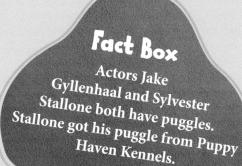

PUGGLE POPULARITY

Puggles became more popular by the early 2000s. Other breeders in the United States had started breeding puggles. People chose the puggle for its appearance and personality. They were drawn to its wrinkly face, its big brown eyes, and its droopy ears. Its friendly and loving personality made the puggle a top pet choice for many dog lovers.

People were also drawn to the puggle because of its small size. Many people living in apartments or small homes prefer small dogs. Celebrities also began getting puggles as pets. When people saw puggles on TV or in magazines with their famous owners, they wanted to get puggles too. People all around the world started breeding puggles to meet this demand.

CHAPTER THREE

ALL ABOUT THE PUGGLE

A puggle's traits can vary from dog to dog. Even siblings from the same litter may differ from one another. Some puggles have more energy and are more playful than others. Some are more cautious than friendly. Despite this variety there are certain traits that people can expect from a puggle.

People choose the puggle because they want a small or medium-sized dog. Most puggles weigh between 15 and 30 pounds (7 and 14 kilograms). They are usually between 10 and 15 inches (25 and 38 centimeters) tall. Height is measured up to the dog's shoulders. Some puggles are even smaller than this. These types of puggles are called toy puggles. Toy puggles are about 10 pounds (5 kilograms) lighter than standard-sized puggles.

Puggles are often playful and have a lot of energy.

13

Both beagles and pugs have short, smooth coats. Puggles **inherit** this type of coat. Similar to their pug parents, puggles can vary in color. Some are black, but most puggles have fawn-colored coats. Fawn isn't a single color but a range of light browns. Within this range, most puggles have golden or tan coats, but some have reddish-brown coats. Some puggles have a black mask of dark fur around their eyes and noses. They get this trait from their pug parents.

PUGGLE PERSONALITIES

Puggles are often very **social**. Their friendly personalities come from both pugs and beagles. They tend to get along with both people and other dogs. This makes puggles good family dogs.

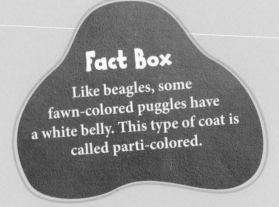

Fact Box

Like beagles, some fawn-colored puggles have a white belly. This type of coat is called parti-colored.

inherit – to get a trait from a parent or ancestor

social – friendly toward people and other dogs

Some puggles have lighter colored coats than others.

Puggles often bark when they get excited, such as when someone knocks on the door. Training could help your puggle bark less often. But puggles can be stubborn and hard to train. They get this trait from both their pug and beagle parents. You will need patience when training your puggle.

Like their beagle relatives, puggles sometimes howl.

ACTIVE PUGGLES

Beagles are hunting dogs. When they smell another animal, they want to follow the animal's scent. Like beagles, puggles often have high energy levels. This trait makes puggles different from pugs, which tend to have low energy levels.

Puggles are often curious. When a puggle is on a walk outside, it will often sniff everything it can. A puggle might decide to follow interesting smells. Puggles sometimes howl while tracking a scent.

Beagles were bred to hunt.

17

CHAPTER FOUR

CARING FOR YOUR PUGGLE

If your family is ready to get a puggle, searching for a responsible breeder is a good place to start. Ask the breeder if the puggle has been to a veterinarian and received the shots it needs. The breeder might also have information about the puggle's family history. This will help you learn if any health conditions run in the puggle's family.

Your family could also try searching for puggles at a local rescue agency or dog shelter. People at the agency or shelter might have information about the puggle's background. The more information you have about your puggle, the better prepared you and your family will be to take care of it.

Puggles need exercise and good care to stay healthy.

Your family can talk to your veterinarian about having your puggle neutered or spayed. Neutering involves removing a part of a male animal's body that helps it make babies. Spaying is a similar process, but it is done for a female. These surgeries keep your dog from having puppies. Dogs that are not spayed or neutered can have many puppies. It can be hard for one family to take care of or find a home for many puppies.

DIET AND EXERCISE

The right diet will help your puggle stay healthy. Your veterinarian can recommend the right type of dog food for your pet and how much to feed it. The right amount of food will depend on your dog's size, its age, and how active it is. Making sure your puggle does not overeat is important. This will help your dog stay at a healthy weight. You should measure out your dog's food at each meal. Active adult puggles typically need about 1 cup (340 grams) of food per day, split into two meals.

Puggle puppies from the same litter may look very similar.

Puggles need at least 30 minutes of exercise each day. You should take your dog on daily walks. You can also play with your dog. Your dog may like to fetch or run.

It is also important to socialize your puggle. This means allowing your puggle to spend time with other people and dogs to learn proper behavior. One way to socialize your dog is to schedule play times with other dogs. The other dogs should be of a similar size and energy level to your puggle. These types of dogs will be most likely to get along well with your puggle.

Agility Training

You can try agility training with your puggle. Agility training is training on a dog obstacle course. There are tunnels for dogs to run through and hurdles to jump over. Dogs weave through lines of cones or poles. There might even be a hoop to jump through. Puggles typically like to run, so your puggle might do well with agility training.

Puggles that are socialized can get along well with other dogs.

HEALTH AND GROOMING

Exercise helps keep your puggle from gaining weight. Less weight means less **stress** on knees and other **joints**. This can help your puggle avoid hip dysplasia. Hip dysplasia is a health problem that is common in both beagles and pugs. In hip dysplasia, the upper leg bone does not fit snugly into the hip joint.

Dogs with short snouts can have breathing problems. Their air passages and nostrils are narrow, which can make breathing difficult. Pugs have short snouts. Puggles tend to have longer snouts than pugs, but they still can have some breathing difficulties. You should make sure exercise is not too hard on your puggle. Your puggle might also pant a lot and have breathing difficulties in hot weather. Keep an eye on your puggle when you play outside together. If your dog pants and seems tired, it is probably time to go inside and cool off.

stress – force and pressure

joint – a point where two bones join together in the body

You should make
sure your puggle has
a comfortable place
to rest.

You should dry off your puggle after it swims to avoid skin infections.

You should brush your puggle's teeth every day. Keeping your dog's teeth clean prevents **tooth decay** and gum problems. Your puggle's nails should be trimmed once every few months. Your veterinarian can teach you how to trim your dog's nails properly.

All dogs need to be groomed. Grooming includes brushing and cleaning your dog's coat. You should brush your dog at least once each week. Although a puggle's coat is short, it sheds a lot. Brushing pulls loose hair out of your dog's coat. As you brush your puggle, you can also check its skin. Puggles often have folds of skin like their pug parents. You should make sure these folds are clean and dry. Puggles can get skin **infections** when moisture and germs get into the folds. These infections are hard to treat, so it is best to prevent them.

 tooth decay – when bacteria destroy the outer surface of a tooth

infection – a condition that occurs when germs such as bacteria and viruses get inside an animal's body

When you groom your puggle, you can also check its eyes. If the corners of its eyes look red and puffy, your puggle might have cherry eye. This is a health problem commonly seen in small dogs. Cherry eye happens when a dog's eyelid begins to swell. The eyelid could get infected if the problem isn't treated.

You should bathe your puggle about once each month. Bathing your puggle more often than this will dry out its skin. Dry skin can make your puggle itchy.

Veterinarians can usually treat a puggle's health issues with medicine or surgery. Sometimes a special diet and exercise can help these problems get better. Your family should take your puggle to the veterinarian at least once a year for a checkup. Puggle puppies need checkups about once every three or four weeks until they reach 16 weeks old. Your veterinarian will give your puggle **vaccination** shots. These shots help protect your puggle against diseases.

vaccination – a shot of a medicine that protects an animal from a disease

Having a pet is a big responsibility, but it is also a lot of fun. Get to know the lovable and energetic puggle. It might be the perfect dog for your family.

Some puggles like to snuggle in blankets.

GLOSSARY

breed (BREED)—a type of dog that has specific traits

breeder (BREED-ur)—someone who brings dogs together so they can breed, or reproduce

infection (in-FEK-shuhn)—a condition that occurs when germs such as bacteria and viruses get inside an animal's body

inherit (in-HAIR-it)—to get a trait from a parent or ancestor

joint (JOYNT)—a point where two bones join together in the body

litter (LIH-tur)—a group of puppies born from the same mother

purebred (PYOOR-bred)—a dog that is the same breed as its parents

social (SOH-shuhl)—friendly toward people and other dogs

stress (STRESS)—force and pressure

tooth decay (TOOTH di-KAY)—when bacteria destroy the outer surface of a tooth

vaccination (VAK-suh-nay-shuhn)—a shot of a medicine that protects an animal from a disease

READ MORE

Gagne, Tammy. *Foxhounds, Coonhounds, and Other Hound Dogs*. Dog Encyclopedias. North Mankato, Minn.: Capstone Press, 2017.

Gray, Susan Heinrichs. *Pugs*. All About Dogs. New York: AV2 by Weigl, 2017.

Potts, Nikki. *Totally Amazing Facts About Dogs*. Mind Benders. North Mankato, Minn.: Capstone Press, 2019.

INTERNET SITES

Use FactHound to find Internet sites related to this book.

Visit www.facthound.com

Just type in 9781543555202 and go.

 **Super-cool stuff!** Check out projects, games and lots more at **www.capstonekids.com**

INDEX